Graphic design and illustrations: Zapp
Story adaptation: Robyn Bryant

© 1994 Tormont Publications Inc.
  338 Saint Antoine St. East
  Montreal, Canada   H2Y 1A3
  Tel. (514) 954-1441
  Fax (514) 954-5086

ISBN 2-89429-506-5

Printed in China

SNOW WHITE

TORMONT

*O*nce upon a time, there lived a beautiful queen. One day, as she was sewing by her window, she pricked her finger with her sewing needle. A drop of blood fell onto the snow on the windowsill.

The red looked so beautiful against the white snow that the queen said: "I wish I had a child with skin as white as snow, lips as red as blood and hair as black as the window frame!"

Soon after, the queen had a baby daughter. The baby had white skin, red lips, and hair as black as ebony, so she named her Snow White.

$\mathcal{U}$nfortunately, the queen died when the child was still a baby. After a while, the king married again. But the new queen was selfish and vain. She had no use for little Snow White at all.

*I*nstead, the new queen spent much of her time gazing at herself in her magic mirror. Each day, she asked the mirror:

"Mirror, mirror, on the wall, who is the fairest one of all?"

The mirror always replied, "You, my queen, are the fairest in the land."

This answer satisfied the queen until the next day, when she would ask again. More than anything, she feared that the mirror would discover someone even more beautiful than her.

*I*n the meantime, Snow White was growing up, and becoming more and more lovely.

One day, the Queen consulted her magic mirror as usual.

"Mirror, mirror, on the wall, who is the fairest one of all?" she asked.

But this time, the mirror answered, "Snow White is the fairest in the land."

The queen was furious! Immediately, she started working on a plan to get rid of Snow White.

The queen called one of the royal huntsmen to a secret meeting. "Take Snow White into the forest and leave her there," she commanded. "And make sure she can never find her way back!"

The huntsman took Snow White to the very edge of the kingdom, and left her alone, deep in the dark forest. Snow White was frightened, and felt like crying. But instead, she decided to find a safe place to spend the night.

*S*he wandered through the woods until she came upon a tiny house. She knocked on the door, but no one answered. So she went in.

Inside, she found a table set with seven plates. Upstairs, she found seven little beds.

Snow White was hungry and tired, so she ate some of the food and then went to sleep on one of the beds.

Later that night, the seven dwarfs who owned the cottage returned, and found Snow White slumbering. She looked so lovely that they decided to let her sleep.

The next morning, the seven dwarfs listened carefully to Snow White's story. "You will be safest if you stay here with us," the dwarfs said.

$\mathcal{W}$hen the seven dwarfs
went off to work, they warned Snow White to
let no one in the house. "The queen is
tricky," they said.

But of course, the queen soon learned from
her magic mirror that Snow White was safe,
and living with the seven dwarfs.

*S*o the queen decided to get rid of Snow White once and for all. She disguised herself as a peasant woman and went to the little house in the woods.

"Apples for sale," she told Snow White.

The apples looked so delicious that Snow White bought one.

$\mathcal{B}$ut the apple had been poisoned. As soon as Snow White bit into it, she fell to the ground.

That night, the dwarfs found Snow White lying on the floor. No breath came from her lips. They thought she was dead.

The seven dwarfs were heartbroken. They could not bring themselves to bury Snow White. Instead, they built her a coffin out of glass, and carried it to the top of the mountain.

From then on, one of the dwarfs stayed always at her side. The years went by. Snow White looked as if she were sleeping.

One day, a handsome prince
happened to be riding his horse
through the forest when he came
upon Snow White in her glass coffin.

$\mathcal{S}$he looked so beautiful that the prince fell in love with her at once.

"Please let me take her back to my castle," the prince begged the seven dwarfs. "I promise to look after her forever. I cannot live without her."

The dwarfs were touched by his loving plea, and agreed.

$\mathcal{B}$ut as the prince's servants were lifting the glass coffin, the piece of apple dislodged from Snow White's throat, and she awoke.

When Snow White saw the handsome prince, she fell in love with him immediately.

Soon after, the prince and Snow White were married, and lived happily ever after.